Sir Quinton Quest Hunts the Jewel

Kaye Umansky and Judy Brown

Collins

Finlay McTrebble and the Fantastic Fertilizer *Scoular Anderson*
Forecast of Fear *Keith Brumpton*
Trouble on the Day *Norma Clarke*
The Curse of Brian's Brick *Andrew Hall*
Bernie Works a Miracle *Leon Rosselson*
Charlie and Biff *Margaret Ryan*
Fergus the Forgetful *Margaret Ryan*
The Man in Shades *Pat Thomson*
Sir Quinton Quest Hunts the Jewel *Kaye Umansky*
Sir Quinton Quest Hunts the Yeti *Kaye Umansky*
The Baked Bean Cure *Philip Wooderson*

10 9 8 7 6 5 4

First published in Great Britain by
A & C Black (Publishers) Ltd 1994
First published by Collins 1994
This impression 1996

Collins is an imprint of HarperCollins*Publishers* Ltd,
77-85 Fulham Palace Road, Hammersmith,
London W6 8JB.

ISBN 0 00 674919-4

Printed and bound in Great Britain by
Omnia Books Ltd, Glasgow

CHAPTER ONE

In which Sir Quinton talks at length about himself, his butler, his wife, his cup and his highly successful last book

Hello there!
I am Sir Quinton Quest, the world famous explorer, here to tell you all about my latest expedition.

First, let me give you a little tour of the mantelpiece in my study.

This is a photograph of my butler, Muggins. Good old Muggins. Jolly sound chap. Absolutely devoted to me, of course. Comes with me on all my expeditions.
This is my wife, Lady Cynthia, who usually remains at home and has a nice quiet time.

This delightful group photograph is of all us SOFE members – SOFE being the Society Of Famous Explorers, for those of you who go round with your heads in paper bags. It was taken at our annual reunion. Jolly important occasion.
You will note the absence of that young upstart Findley Ffoothold, my explorer rival. Probably off making a pop record or modelling the latest "in" climbing wear, I shouldn't wonder. Just as well, really. We don't want his sort in SOFE. Well, I don't, anyway.

Pshaugh! Findley Ffoothold indeed! Can't stand the chap! I'll waste no more words on him, the conceited, insolent, brash, cocky, swaggering, shameless, offhand, loutish, overfamiliar, thoroughly objectionable young bounder!

Instead,
we'll go on to **THIS**.

The coveted
Explorer Of The
Year Challenge Cup.

Every year this highly desirable trophy is awarded to the explorer who has demonstrated the most grit, determination, courage in the face of great odds and so on. All the explorers I know would cheerfully sell their grannies to the Eskimos for the chance to possess this cup.

But they don't get the chance.
Tell them, Cynthia.

Mmmm? Tell them what, dear?
You know.
Oh...Quinny's won it six years running, isn't he lucky?
Skilful you mean. Luck doesn't come into it.

Silly woman. Yes, for six years running I have won this remarkable trophy. Last year, you may remember, I went to the Himalayas on my famed Yeti hunt.

The book I wrote about it has naturally been a sensational success, and is regarded by many as a classic. Top of the Best Seller list for three weeks running.

Best Seller List

1. **My Hunt for the Yeti – Sir Quinton Quest**
2. Investigating Live Volcanoes – Professor Egbert von Fuelhardy-Nitt
3. Looking Good On Mountains – Findley Ffoothold
4. Treasures of the Deep – Ivor Snorkel
5. Dangerous Waters – Roxanne Piranhafish
6. The Cold North – Jilly Fingers
7. Deserts Revisited – Miles O'Sand & Dee Oddcamel
8. Our Weekend In The Country – Rosa Fields and Teresa Plenty
9. Flying Blue Pigs In The Desert – Amy Raj
10. Beginners Guide to Jungle Insects – Amos Keeto

As you can see, it even outsold the mind – blowing *Investigating Live Volcanoes* by my old friend Professor Egbert von Fuelhardy-Nitt, the highly respected archaeologist, biologist, scientist, volcanologist and all-round clever Dick.

How could I follow that? What could I do next to demonstrate my incredible bravery, excellent qualities of leadership and amazing powers of endurance? I knew I needed to mount an expedition to somewhere to find out something or other.

For the life of me, I couldn't think of anything . . .

CHAPTER TWO

In which Sir Quinton continues to rack his brains, Findley Ffoothold gets in first, Lady Cynthia receives a recipe and an unexpected letter arrives

For weeks I racked my brains, but came up with nothing, despite eating fish till they swam out of my ears. Good for the brains, fish.

I confess I became really worried when that loathsome young whelp Ffoothold called a Press Conference and announced *his* latest idea.

Much to my disgust, the young pup's stupid face was splashed all over the front page of the *Daily Explorer* yet again.

THE DAILY EXPLORER

Scoop!
Findley's Done It Again!

Findley Ffoothold (23) the dashing young adventurer, is planning an assault on the dreaded North face of Mount Killinmalegso – *by Yak!*

'I think this new expedition is incredibly exciting,' enthused the handsome young explorer. 'I firmly believe that this year the Explorer Of The Year Challenge Cup will be mine, all mine! It's time that boring old twit Quinton Quest was given a run for his money. I've already got the Yak. It's name is Gerald . . . blah blah . . .'

The cheek of it! Shameless young jackanapes, how dare he! I wrote and complained, of course. Several letters, all under different names.

Dear Sir,
Please, please, no more Findley Ffoothold! Instead, what about a big photo of that gorgeous hunk Sir Quinton Quest??
Quest Fan, Bournemouth.

must protest
wasting spare
wonderful
Quest

dare that show off Ffoothold
say what he did about that fine explorer, Sir Quinton Quest. I am amazed you print such lies. I am cancelling my subscription forthwith.
Outraged, Berwick-Upon-Tweed.

Furious,

The trouble was, in my heart of hearts, I knew that Ffoothold had hit upon a good idea. It was new. It was different. It was terribly dangerous. It had animal interest. No one had ever thought of doing it before. Mount Killinmalegso by yak, eh? I wished I'd thought of it.

I simply had to come up with something better – and quick!

And then it happened!

I inspected the letter.

Immediately, I recognised the writing. It was from my old friend Professor Egbert von Fuelhardy-Nitt – author of *Investigating Live Volcanoes.* What a surprise. It had been some time since I had heard from old 'Eggy', as I always used to call him at school. Short for egghead, of course. Jolly good chap, Eggy. Always shared his tucker box and let me copy his maths homework.

Well, well. Old Eggy, eh? I wondered what he wanted. I knew he was on an important archaeological dig:

Professor Egbert von Fuelhardy-Nitt (63) departed today for Egypt, where he is planning a highly secret, incredibly important archaeological dig.

Eagerly, I tore the envelope open. Inside was a short note.

Oasis Hotel

Dear Questy

Am on ze verge of important discovery. Unfortunately, got blown up by volcano again last veek. I haf vun or two injuries vich make it hard for me to get about. Urgently need friend I can trust. Please come out immediately. Am staying at ze Oasis Hotel, Pyramid Avenue, Cairo, Egypt.

Eggy

P.S. Food awful. Kindly brink P.G. Tips and German sausage.

P.P.S. And a spade.

Eureka! This was it! This was exactly what I was looking for. I would place my expertise at good old Eggy's disposal, be present at the unveiling of the important discovery, take him out his teabags and sausage, take all the credit – and, naturally, win the Challenge Cup for the seventh year running!

What a wonderful idea! I broke the news immediately. First to Muggins . . .

. . . and then to Lady Cynthia.
That's when the first fly landed in the ointment, so to speak.

Ah, but I haven't seen Agnes for ages. We were at school together, you know. I knew her when she was plain simple Agnes Tupperware, long before she married your friend and became a Fuelhardy-Nitt. We can catch up on old times while you and the Professor talk about boring old exploring.

The one thing We Explorers learn is how to take the rough with the smooth. I said nothing more and went off to make up my list of essential supplies.

CHAPTER THREE

In which Sir Quinton, Lady Cynthia and Muggins arrive at the Oasis Hotel and meet with their friends, the Fuelhardy-Nitts – but not before attracting attention from the wrong quarter

I will not trouble you with the grim details of our journey, except to say that I will be writing some pretty strong letters of complaint to British Rail, Camel Airlines and Sphinx Cab Hire, I can tell you.

Instead, let me skip straight to the moment when we arrived at the Oasis Hotel.

At last! Journey's end. Travel-stained and thirsty, we alighted from the death machine that called itself a taxi. It was hot, darned hot. So hot, I undid the top button of my safari jacket and Lady Cynthia removed one of her cardigans.

Once inside, I made straight for reception, where I introduced myself.

I am Sir Quinton Quest, the world-famous explorer, you've probably heard of me. I shall require the best room in the hotel with a huge cool fan and en suite teasmade for her ladyship and myself, and a small cheap stiflingly hot cupboard for my butler.

Then . . .

There they were! Our old friends, the Fuelhardy-Nitts!

And that was the last I saw of Cynthia. Just as well. She would only have got in the way.

I was shocked to see poor old Eggy. He really had been in the wars.

Once my poor old friend was settled in a shady corner, I ordered Muggins to go and get us two Oasis Specials with extra ice. Being a thoughtful sort of employer, I told him to treat himself to a small packet of dry biscuits; something to munch on later while he was carrying the bags up to our rooms. Off he went, looking very grateful, and Eggy began his story.

CHAPTER FOUR

In which Professor von Fuelhardy-Nitt reveals the exciting, mysterious and ultimately tragic events of the past weeks

'It all began' (said the Professor), 'on zat fateful day ven I am in ze Explorers' Library . . .

Zere vos I, rummagink around in ze archives, ven vot am I discoverink but loose brick in ze vall!'

'Behind vos secret compartment! Vundebar! I am much excited to see zat it is containink a crumplink book!

It vos clear zat I had stumbled on sumpzink of earth-shattering importance for all mankind.

Naturally, I am vantink to keep mine find to mineself for a bit. All mankind could vait. I sneaked ze book out and took it home.

'Oh no. It vos all in hieroglyphics. Luckily, I haf mine copy of zat useful little book, *Janet and John Learn Hieroglyphics*. I get myself big pot of coffee and prepare to burn ze midnight oil.

Zis vos even better zan I had hoped! Ze book vos all about a mysterious Egyptian queen by ze name of Tutataxi! And guess vot? She is none uzzer zan ze cousin of Cleopatra, zat vell-known and highly glamorous Queen of ze Nile!

Vat a fascinatink read! I couldn't put it down. Vot a tale of intrigue and jealousy.'

'Having a very bad temper und terrible dress sense as vell as not brushink ze teeth much, Tutataxi voz alvays overlooked in favour of her famous cousin.

Cleopatra voz very pretty and popular and had loads of friends and got invited to all ze discos. In ze meantime, Tutataxi skulked in ze shadows, gnashink her horrible teeth in jealous fury.

By popular demand, Cleopatra became Queen of ze Nile.'

'Tutataxi vos fobbed off viz ze River Dribble, a small, crocodile-infested tributary running six metres into ze desert before peterink out in a muddy puddle. Tutataxi could take no more. Her jealousy levels reached all-time high.

She svore to avenge herself. Now comes ze best part of ze story.

Vun day Tutataxi vos thumink through old magazines in ze dentist's vaitink room, vunderink how to get her revenge. Suddenly, vot does she see but an exclusive offer for ze vorld's biggest uncut diamond! She knew that Cleopatra loved jewellery and had ze best collection of rare jewels in ze whole of Egypt.'

'Tutataxi filled in ze coupon and sent off for ze diamond straightaway.

FIT FOR A QUEEN
ATTENTION ALL COLLECTORS!
Exclusive offer, world's biggest uncut diamond, be the envy of your friends.

Simply cut out coupon below.

Yes! Please rush me my exclusive uncut diamond immediately if not sooner! I enclose an enormous amount of money.

Name ....
Address ....
....

Ven it arrived, the jewel vos even better zan Tutataxi is expectink' (continued the Professor). 'Ze second she saw it, Tutataxi vent rushink off to Cleopatra's palace.'

'Cleopatra vos furious.

Cleopatra said she voz never speakink to her again and Tutataxi said see if she cared and somevun's dress got torn.'

'Excitedly, I turned ze page to find out vot happened next.

Horrors! Zere is no more. Ze last vital page voz missink. Vot a disappointment. Mein heart sank. Vos I destined never to know vot had become of ze diamond?

Anxiously I examined ze book, hopink to find a clue. Zen, to my joy, vot am I findink but some ancient pieces of papyrus, cunningly secreted inside ze cover of ze book.'

'Zese old papers told me all I vished to know. A map showink ze location of Tutataxi's tomb – a cross-section of ze burial chamber – everysink! So. I decide to come to Egypt, find ze tomb, recover ze jewel, present it to ze Explorers' Museum, get my photograph in ze paper, write a book about it and make a lot of money. But zis vos not to be.'

'Before ve set off for Egypt, a telegram arrived.'

To: Professor Egbert von Fuelhardy-Nitt.

Come to South America immediately. Stop. Volcano erupting. Stop. Big, noisy one. Stop. You'll love it. Stop. A well-wisher.

'Quinny, Quinny, vat vas I to do? You know me. Viz some people it's stamps. Viz me, it's volcanoes. Volcanoes are my passion. I can say viz pride zat I haf been blown up by almost every important volcano in ze vorld. Except zis vun. I had to go. It vas as simple as zat. Ze vife haf a bit to say, of course.'

This is the last one, the very last one.
Don't vorry, dear, I'm sure it von't be dangerous.

'Anyvay, here I am, on ze verge of an important discovery and my injuries are makink it impossible to organise ze Dig. Zat is vy I send for you. You are ze only vun I can trust. Vill you help, old friend? Vill you help me to discover ze lost jewel of Tutataxi?'

Well, what could I say?
Leave it to me Eggy, I'm your man.

O happy day! This is it, O Abdul! The Big One. Now we can use our dastardly plan!
You are right, O Haroun. What was our dastardly plan again?
To follow these madmen steal this ancient jewel and become rich beyond our wildest dreams.
EAT AT ALI'S
My cup of happiness is running over.
But not for long It's your turn to fill the camel's bucket.
I'm not running on empty.
CAMEL FOO

CHAPTER FIVE

In which our heroes do a spot of map-reading and find out about the curse

We set off into the desert at dawn the following day. Muggins drove and I, of course, did the map-reading. Poor old Eggy made himself as comfortable as he could in the back.

Left at the next sand dune and sharp right by the next vulture.

After driving around for several hours, I began to suspect that something was wrong with the map. I was right! It was upside down! That's the trouble with sand. It can be confusing.

We retraced our route. This took several more hours. The midday sun beat down relentlessly. We did what we could to keep our spirits up. We sang songs. We played word games.

And then Eggy amused us by telling us all about some ridiculous little curse that Tutataxi had set up.

At last, we reached the spot.

Once Muggins had unpacked, I instructed him to get on with the digging. No point in wasting time.

CHAPTER SIX

In which Queen Tutataxi's lost tomb is found and investigated with initially disappointing results

At long last, we struck gold! This was it! The entrance to Tutataxi's tomb.

I suppose I should have woken poor Eggy to share this very special moment. But after thinking about it deeply for a second or two, I decided not to bother. Why wake a sick man who needs his sleep? Besides, this could well be the find of the century. My blood was up! The tomb was beckoning to me. This was my big moment. In I went.

Muggins was making a ridiculous fuss about the curse. I reminded him that the curse is only supposed to fall upon the first person to enter the inner chamber. Goodness knows where *that* was.

It was dark, damp, and smelly in the tomb. After a time my torch battery began to flicker – and suddenly, it went out!

I could hear Muggins blundering about in the dark.

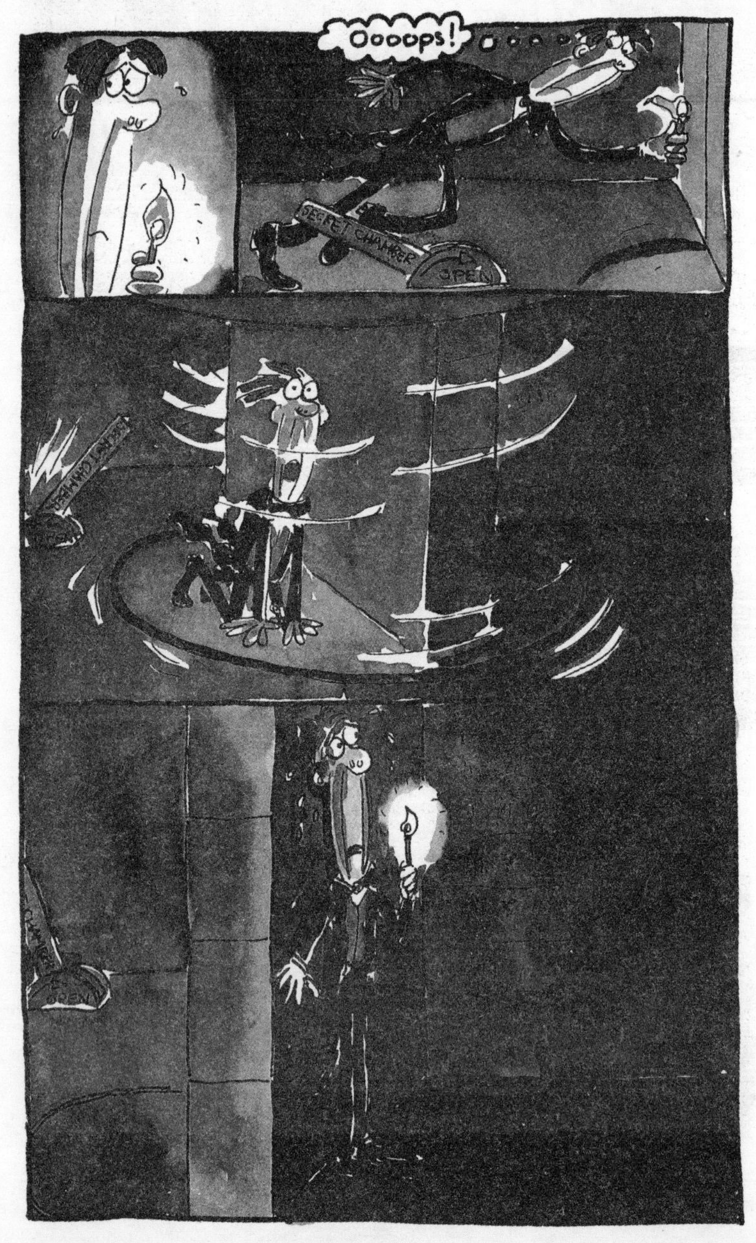

Did you see what just happened to the penguin?
Now! Now's our chance, O Haroun. The jewel is within our grasp.

Hold your camels, O Abdul. First let us hasten back to get torches, ropes, pizza, a spare vest - anything that might be useful. We must be prepared to make a quick getaway.

CHAPTER SEVEN

In which Sir Quinton sets things rolling

I got tired of waiting for Muggins. I left the tomb and returned to the tent, passing Eggy on the way. He was still sleeping like a baby. Really! I was beginning to feel that the only one with any get-up-and-go on this expedition was myself!

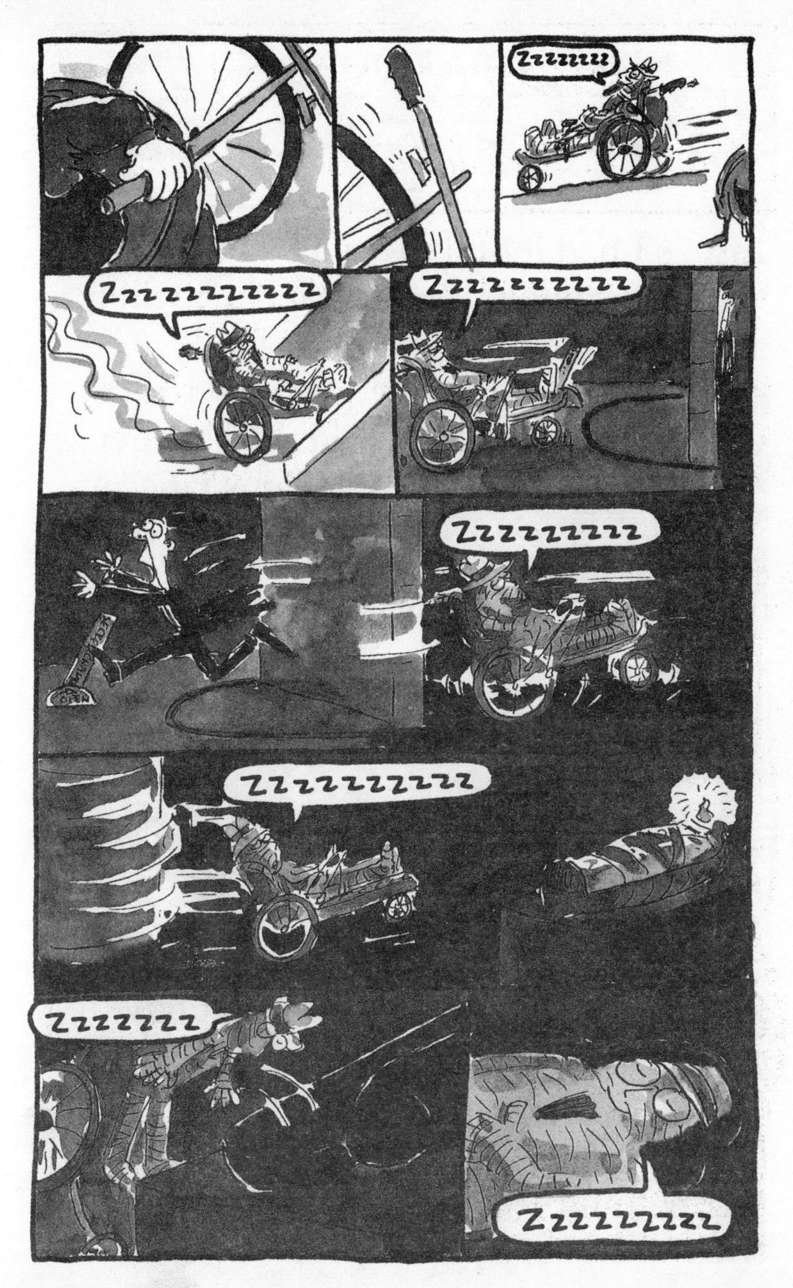
Zzzzzzzz
Zzzzzzzzzzz
Zzzzzzzzzzz
Zzzzzzzzzz
Zzzzzzzzzzz
Zzzzzzz
Zzzzzzzzzz

Just as I had found the spare battery, Muggins came racing up babbling wildly about being shut up in the inner chamber, convinced he was now the victim of the curse. I asked what evidence he had to support his ridiculous fancies.

He pointed out that he was currently being attacked by a plague of locusts.

This was true, but one must put up with these little inconveniences when one is on a serious expedition. I told him to use some insect repellent. I had other things on my mind. For example – **where was the Professor**?

CHAPTER EIGHT

In which Abdul and Haroun get the jewel – and a very nasty shock

Do you hear a strange rapping noise coming from this mummy case, O Haroun, or is it me?
RAP
RAP
BINGO
Vot time is it? Is it morning? Vere am I? Who are zese sinister men?
AAAAARGH!
Help! Mummy!
Run for it!
Whatever happens, O Haroun, do not drop the jewel.

As I returned from my fruitless search for the missing Professor something caught my eye! Two strange figures came running out of the tomb! What's more, to my amazement, who should come hobbling out in hot pursuit but the Professor!

Luckily I knew what to do in an emergency.

CHAPTER NINE

In which Abdul and Haroun hasten back to town and our heroes have a series of unfortunate mishaps

I shall never forget that chase across the desert – the hot, searing sun – the glare of the dazzling white sands – the hopeful croaks of the circling vultures – the roar of the overheated jeep's engines – Muggins' terrible driving . . .

I really don't know how it is you seem so accident prone this expedition, Muggins.

It wasn't long before we had to stop to pick up poor old Eggy. He had lost both crutches and not surprisingly, his bandages were unravelling.

'Never mind, old chap,' I told him kindly.

'You did your best and you are, after all, a sick man. Hop on in, and we'll soon catch up with those rascals.'

But it wasn't as simple as that.

If there was one rusty nail in the entire desert, you could be sure that Muggins would drive over it.

And all this time the thieves were getting further and further away. Doubtless they were hastening back to town, where they would sell the jewel to the highest bidder.

Whew! Made it.
That was a close thing.
EAT AT ALI'S
(HAIR STYLING
Now what do we do, O Haroun, sell the jewel?
All in good time, O Abdul. First we must find a way of putting these madmen off our trail once and for all.
You speak wisely. But how?
DAZZLE YOUR FRIENDS
FAKE JEWELS MADE TO ORDER WHILE U WAIT
REASONABLE RATES
KNOCK THREE TIMES AND ASK FOR
FATIMA THE FORGER
(HAIR STYLING EXTRA)
Sometimes this coincidence thing gets taken too far, don't you think O, Abdul?

CHAPTER TEN

In which there is a squabble, a vision, and a very unpleasant trek across the desert

I think that our journey across the desert on the trail of those two rogues was possibly one of the worst in my entire experience.

Talking of prizes made me think of the Challenge Cup. I had a horrific vision in which that odious Findley Ffoothold and his confounded yak won the Cup instead of me!

Aaargh no!
Anything but that!

I spurred Muggins on to greater efforts.

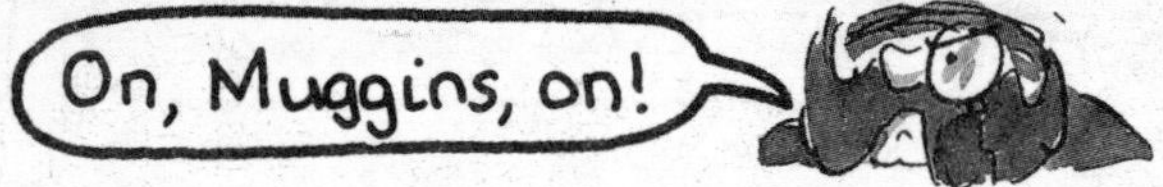

On, Muggins, on!

Across the white hot sands we toiled, ever onwards, never resting, eking out our last drops of water and only stopping for lunch and the occasional cup of tea.
And at long last, thanks to my amazing leadership, our battered party limped into town.

CHAPTER ELEVEN

In which our heroes arrive in town, have a wash and brush-up and set out for a final showdown

We caused quite a stir amongst the locals. I confess I felt rather annoyed. I'm a serious explorer and serious explorers like to be taken seriously.

No sense in letting standards drop. Muggins' suit was badly in need of a press, and the Professor's bandages were a disgrace to the health service.

I decided we should return to our hotel for a badly needed wash and brush-up before setting out once again on the villains' trail.

I had rather hoped that Cynthia would be anxiously awaiting my return, but it was not to be. No sign of Agnes either. I simply can't imagine what these women do all day long.

There's nothing quite like a long, cool shower to make one feel like a new man. I'm sure the others felt the same.

Now comes the most astonishing thing of all. No sooner had we strode forth from the hotel, than those thieves actually shot out of a nearby alleyway and ran across our path! What luck!

Would you believe it! Yet another extraordinary stroke of luck! So eager were the villains to get away that they actually dropped their ill-gotten gains! There it lay, this glorious ancient jewel, glittering in the dust. What an incredible sight. Slowly, I bent and picked it up.

At last! Tutataxi's precious diamond was mine.

Have you ever noticed how, at the moment of triumph, something always happens to spoil it?

CHAPTER TWELVE

In which everything gets neatly sorted out to everyone's satisfaction – almost

I cannot describe to you the pride I felt when I finally presented the jewel to a grateful representative of the Cairo branch of the Explorers' Museum. The Professor insisted on being at the presentation ceremony too, which slightly cramped my style – but I think nobody was in any doubt about who did all the work and took all the risks. Not after my speech, anyway.

A very satisfactory ending to the expedition, I'm sure you will agree. Just to add to my pleasure, when I got back to England I heard that Findley Ffoothold had dismally failed to conquer the North face of Mount Killinmalegso. A difference of opinion with the yak, apparently.

So the good news is that the Explorer Of The Year Challenge Cup will definitely be mine again – for the seventh year running! And all thanks to the lost jewel of Tutataxi.

Sometimes I wonder about Muggins.